SILENT NIGHT

A Christmas Horror

D. DECKKER

Dinsu Books

ISBN-13: 9798345647929

Cover design by: D. DECKKER
Printed in the United States of America

For Subhashini and Sasha

To my beloved wife, Subhashini,
Your unwavering support and love light my darkest hours.

To my dearest daughter, Sasha,
Your laughter and wonder remind me that even amidst shadows,
joy endures.

This book is for you both, my heart and my home.

– D. Deckker

CONTENTS

PREFACE

In the stillness of winter, where snow blankets the world in deceptive serenity, a tale of friendship, fear, and resilience unfolds. A group of friends ventures into the woods, seeking laughter and escape, only to find themselves ensnared in an ancient darkness. This is not a story about the innocence of snowfall or the warmth of a crackling fire—it is about the shadows that lurk just beyond the edge of the light, the whispers carried by the wind, and the unseen eyes watching from the void.

Here, the bonds of trust are tested, courage is forged in the crucible of terror, and the fine line between myth and reality dissolves. As you turn the pages, prepare to leave behind the comfort of the familiar and step into a world where the cold bites deeper, the night stretches longer, and survival demands more than mere endurance.

Welcome to a chilling journey into the heart of winter's darkness. **Silent Night** beckons you to enter, but be warned—not all who venture out of the storm return unscathed.

CHAPTER 1: SNOWBOUND

The car rumbled along the snowy highway, music blasting from the speakers as laughter filled the cabin. Mia leaned over the center console, her phone aimed perfectly to capture her friends. Always the documenter of the group, Mia loved capturing moments, her easygoing nature and creative eye making her the unofficial historian of their adventures. "Say 'blizzard buddies!'" she called out, the camera pointed at the back seat where Tyler and Kayla were bundled in scarves and hats.

"Blizzard buddies!" they yelled in unison, striking exaggerated poses as Jason, the driver, let out a loud groan. He rolled his eyes but smiled, his gloved hands gripping the steering wheel. He couldn't help but feel a mix of amusement and mild annoyance at their antics—he loved his friends, but sometimes their endless photo sessions tested his patience. Sam, sitting beside Mia in the front seat, laughed while checking her phone, scrolling through their posts.

"This is going to be epic," Sam said, clicking her tongue in approval at the selfies and videos that Mia had already posted to their stories. They had been talking about this winter getaway for weeks—a few days away from school, from parents, and from the pressures of life, just to have fun before the holidays. A cozy cabin in the woods sounded like the perfect pre-Christmas retreat.

The car's tires crunched through the thickening snow, and the music seemed to blend with the sound of the wind that was picking up outside. The road twisted, leading deeper into the woods.

"Look at that snow," Tyler said, his eyes wide as he pressed his nose against the window. "It's like Narnia out here."

"Yeah, but with way more Instagram filters," Kayla added, grinning as she took a snap of the view. She turned to Jason. "How much longer, captain? It feels like we've been driving forever."

Jason glanced at his phone, his GPS barely functioning. "Uh, says about ten more minutes... if we don't get lost."

Mia smirked. "Are you sure you know where you're going, Jason? I don't want to end up in some horror movie trope where the car breaks down in the middle of nowhere."

"Relax, Mia," Jason replied, giving her a confident grin. "I've got this under control. Besides, what's the worst that could happen?"

The group collectively groaned. "Dude, never say that," Sam said, shaking her head. "That's how you jinx us." A slight unease settled over them, the kind that comes when a joke feels just a bit too real, but they quickly brushed it off.

A few minutes later, as if on cue, the wind outside picked up dramatically. The sky, already gray, darkened further as the snow started falling heavily, swirling in aggressive patterns across the windshield. The cheerful atmosphere in the car grew tense as Jason slowed down, squinting to see through the thickening flurry.

"Whoa, okay, this is getting serious," Jason muttered. He flicked the windshield wipers on high, but they were struggling to keep up. The GPS blinked off, losing signal.

"Are we almost there?" Kayla asked, a hint of worry in her voice now.

Mia checked her phone. No signal. She exchanged a look with Sam, who shrugged. "It's fine, we're probably super close. Let's just keep going," Sam said, though she too sounded less sure.

Finally, through the blinding snow, they spotted the dark outline of a building—a small cabin, half-buried under the thick blanket of snow. It looked almost eerie, as if it had been forgotten by time, its shadowy form giving off an unsettling, lonely vibe that made them hesitate for just a moment. Relief swept through the car as Jason carefully pulled up the driveway, tires slipping slightly before they came to a stop. The group sighed collectively as they piled out of the car, each of them grabbing bags and supplies from the trunk.

"Welcome to our winter wonderland," Tyler announced, stretching his arms wide as snowflakes settled on his hat. He hurried to the door, Mia right behind him. She was filming again, capturing Tyler struggling with the key.

"Come on, man, it's freezing out here!" she laughed, her breath visible in the icy air.

Finally, Tyler managed to open the door, and they all rushed inside, stomping the snow from their boots. The interior was rustic and old-fashioned—wooden beams across the ceiling, a large stone fireplace, and dusty furniture covered in white sheets.

"Okay, this is actually kind of creepy," Kayla said, wrinkling her nose and glancing around the dimly lit cabin. She shifted her weight from one foot to the other, her fingers fidgeting with the edge of her scarf as if to ward off a growing sense of unease. She pulled out her phone and turned on the flashlight, casting long shadows across the room.

"Nah, it's got character," Sam said, tossing her backpack onto the couch and pulling one of the sheets off. Dust flew everywhere, and Jason coughed loudly, waving his hand in front of his face.

"Let's get a fire going," Jason suggested, moving toward the fireplace. "Someone find the WiFi—I'm not about to go without connection for the whole weekend."

Mia laughed. "Good luck with that. Something tells me this place was built before the internet even existed."

Kayla rolled her eyes and held up her phone, spinning in a slow circle. "No bars. Great. I hope nobody needed to call home."

"Oh, come on," Tyler said, grinning. "We came here to disconnect, right? Embrace the snowstorm, the lack of WiFi... it'll be like a digital detox." He waggled his fingers in the air dramatically, making Mia giggle.

"Yeah, yeah, but I still want hot chocolate," Sam said, heading toward the small kitchen area. "Let's get this place warmed up."

Jason worked on lighting the fire while Kayla helped Sam unpack their supplies. Mia and Tyler explored the rest of the cabin, finding old knick-knacks—rusty lanterns, faded postcards, and small carved figurines—that seemed to whisper of forgotten lives. Dusty photos of people who had clearly lived here ages ago stared back at them from cracked frames, their expressions solemn, as if guarding the secrets of the past. The place had an almost eerie quality, like it was suspended in time.

"Look at this," Tyler said, holding up an old black-and-white photo. It showed a family standing outside the cabin—parents, kids, all staring straight at the camera with somber expressions that seemed almost unnatural, their eyes hollow and their mouths set in rigid lines. It was as if they were being forced to pose, their faces devoid of any warmth or joy. The longer Mia looked, the more unsettling it felt, like the family was trying to convey some unspoken warning. "These people look like they hated Christmas."

Mia shivered, not just from the cold. "Yeah, let's put that away. It's kind of freaking me out."

They returned to the living room, where a fire was now crackling warmly in the fireplace. The orange glow filled the room, and the friends settled in, huddling under blankets they had brought. Sam handed out mugs of hot chocolate, and the atmosphere lightened again as they took turns roasting marshmallows over the fire.

"Okay, so here's the plan," Jason said, leaning back with his mug. "We chill tonight, watch some movies, and just relax. Tomorrow, we'll explore the woods a bit, maybe build a snowman or two. Sound good? Just us, the snow, and a whole lot of quiet. No one around for miles, especially with this storm closing in."

Everyone nodded, and Kayla added, "And we should do a TikTok dance challenge. Imagine the views we'd get doing it in a blizzard."

"You and your TikToks," Mia teased. "But fine, I'm in. As long as Tyler doesn't try to sabotage it like last time."

Tyler feigned innocence, holding up his hands. "Hey, I just added my own flavor to it. You all are just jealous of my moves."

The group laughed, the earlier tension melting away as they fell into easy conversation. Outside, the wind howled, rattling the windows, but inside they felt safe—warm and isolated from the rest of the world.

Hours passed, and the storm outside only intensified. Snow piled up against the windows, and the wind howled like a living thing. They took turns sharing ghost stories, the flickering fire adding an extra layer of creepiness to the tales.

"Okay, okay, my turn," Mia said, her eyes twinkling as she leaned forward. "Once upon a time, there were five friends stuck in a creepy old cabin in the middle of a snowstorm..."

"Really, Mia?" Jason interrupted, raising an eyebrow. "That's literally our situation right now."

"Exactly!" Mia said, her voice dropping to a whisper. "And they had no idea... that they weren't alone."

Kayla shivered dramatically. "Stop, you're gonna freak me out for real."

Mia just smiled, but before she could continue, the room went pitch dark. The fire still flickered, but every light in the cabin had gone out. The sudden darkness felt thick and suffocating, as if the shadows were pressing in on them. The temperature seemed to drop instantly, and an uneasy silence settled, broken only by the crackling of the fire.

"Whoa, what the heck?" Sam said, her voice laced with surprise.

"Power outage," Jason said, pulling out his phone and turning on the flashlight. "Must be the storm."

"Great," Tyler muttered. "No lights, no cell service, and it's like zero degrees outside. This just keeps getting better."

Kayla huddled closer to the fire. "As long as the power comes back on soon, I'll survive."

Jason stood up, his flashlight beam cutting through the darkness. "I'll go check the fuse box. Maybe we can get the lights back on."

"Want me to come with?" Mia offered, her bravado from earlier slightly shaken.

"Nah, I got it. Be right back," Jason said, disappearing into the hallway, the light bobbing until it vanished around the corner.

The others sat in silence for a moment, the sound of the wind outside now more prominent without the hum of electricity. Sam shifted uncomfortably, her eyes darting to the dark windows. "Anyone else feel like this is how horror movies start?"

"Stop," Kayla said, giving her a playful shove. "We're fine. It's just a power outage. Jason will get it sorted."

Mia nodded, though she couldn't shake the unease that had settled over her. She picked up her phone, staring at the screen—still no signal. She let out a breath and forced a smile. "Hey, Tyler, tell us another story while we wait. Something not about our current predicament."

Tyler opened his mouth to respond, but just then, a loud thud echoed from somewhere deep in the house. Everyone froze, eyes wide as they glanced at each other.

"Did... did you guys hear that?" Sam whispered, his voice barely a breath above silence. The words trembled in the chilled air, each syllable punctuated by the faint, rhythmic creak of floorboards settling somewhere in the darkness. His wide eyes flicked to the shadowy corners, where shapes seemed to shift and pulse, almost alive. A low hum of tension settled around them, thick and heavy, making the hair on his arms prickle. The distant rustle—so soft it was almost imagined—scratched through the silence, sending a shiver that rippled down his spine like ice water.

"Probably just Jason messing around," Kayla said, though her voice lacked conviction.

Mia swallowed, her gaze fixed on the hallway where Jason had disappeared. The fire crackled, the only sound in the otherwise silent room. She tried to laugh, but it came out shaky. "Yeah, he's probably just trying to scare us. Typical Jason."

But deep down, a part of her wasn't so sure.

CHAPTER 2: THE FIRST NIGHT

The wind howled outside, a constant wail that seemed to rattle the windows with every gust. The cold seeped into their bones, turning their limbs heavy and sluggish. The chill felt relentless, making their joints ache and their fingers numb. Each breath sent a painful sting through their lungs, and the air hung thick and damp, adding to the suffocating atmosphere., and each gust carried an unsettling sense of isolation. The temperature inside the lodge had dropped significantly since the power had gone out, forcing the group to huddle together in the dim light cast by their phone flashlights. Jason had gone out earlier to try and fix the power, but he couldn't. Now, he flicked his light across the room, the beam catching on old furniture and cobwebbed corners. A chill ran down his spine, and he couldn't shake the feeling that something was watching them from the shadows. The shadows danced across the walls, creating an eerie atmosphere that none of them could shake.

"Okay, this isn't funny anymore," Kayla said, crossing her arms, her breath fogging slightly. The cold seemed to seep into her bones, making her muscles tense, and she shivered involuntarily, her discomfort growing with each passing moment. "If this is some elaborate prank, I swear I'm going to murder you, Jason."

Jason gave her an incredulous look, holding his hands up in mock surrender. "Kayla, I've told you a hundred times, it's not me. Do you really think I'd go through all this trouble just to freak you guys out?"

Mia shivered slightly, wrapping a blanket tighter around herself. "He's right. This doesn't feel like a prank. It's maybe the storm is making everything sound worse than it is, but what if it isn't? What if there's something else out there? I can't help but feel there's more to it—like we're not alone here.." She glanced at the windows where the snow was piling up. The whole scene felt like they were completely cut off from the rest of the world.

"Yeah, well, whatever it is, it's getting on my nerves," Kayla replied, rolling her eyes. The scratching at the door had stopped, but a new sound—soft footsteps, almost like a child's—echoed faintly from down the hallway.

Tyler, sitting by the fire, which was now just embers, raised his head, his brows furrowed. The dying fire mirrored the group's dwindling sense of safety, the warmth and security fading along with the flames. "Did anyone else hear that?" he whispered.

"Hear what?" Sam asked, clearly unnerved but trying to keep her cool.

Tyler pointed down the dark hallway that led to the back rooms of the lodge. "Footsteps. I swear I just heard footsteps."

Mia let out a nervous laugh, trying to lighten the mood. "Okay, now you're all just messing with me, right?" But her voice lacked conviction.

Jason shook his head, shining his light toward the hallway. "No one's messing with anyone. Let's just check it out. Probably just something falling over."

Kayla snorted, clearly unimpressed. "Yeah, great idea, Jason. Go right ahead and walk into the creepy hallway. I'll stay right here, thank you very much."

But Jason was already on his feet, his phone flashlight leading the way. Mia hesitated for a second before standing up as well. "I'll come with you," she said, her voice more confident than she felt. Tyler sighed and got up too, not wanting to be left behind.

The hallway stretched out in front of them, the beam from Jason's flashlight barely penetrating the darkness. Jason felt an involuntary shiver run down his spine, the oppressive silence making him feel like eyes were watching him from the shadows. The wooden floor creaked under their steps, the sound echoing through the lodge as they made their way further in. Mia walked close to Jason, her eyes darting from side to side. She couldn't shake the feeling that they were being watched. In her mind, she pictured a shadowy figure lurking just beyond the edges of the light, its unseen eyes tracking their every move.

"There's nothing here, see?" Jason said, his voice low. He opened the door to one of the rooms, revealing nothing but dusty furniture and old, faded curtains. He turned back to Mia and Tyler, shrugging. "It's just an old lodge."

Mia let out a sigh of relief, though it didn't completely shake the feeling of unease that had settled in her chest. Just as they turned to head back to the living room, there was a sudden loud bang from behind them. It sounded like something had been slammed shut.

Mia jumped, her flashlight beam jerking wildly as she let out a small scream. Tyler swore under his breath, while Jason turned quickly, shining his light back toward the end of the hallway. The door they had just checked stood open, swaying slightly as if caught by a breeze. An unexpected chill emanated from the room, and there was a faint, musty scent, like something long forgotten had just been disturbed.

"Okay, what was that?" Tyler asked, his voice shaking slightly.

Jason took a deep breath, forcing a smile. He hesitated for a moment, his eyes flickering to the hallway before he spoke again. "Probably just the wind. It's storming pretty hard outside, remember?"

But Mia wasn't convinced. She felt the hairs on her arms standing up, her instincts screaming at her that something was wrong. She pointed her flashlight down the hallway again, and for just a split second, she thought she saw something—a shadow, something moving just out of sight.

"Did you see that?" she whispered, her eyes wide.

"See what?" Jason asked, his voice tinged with unease.

"I swear I saw something," Mia said, stepping back, her heart pounding. She couldn't tell if it was just her imagination playing tricks on her, but something about this place felt off.

"Maybe we should just head back to the living room," Tyler suggested, his voice shaky. "This is getting too creepy."

Jason nodded, and they all quickly made their way back, none of them daring to look back down the dark hallway. When they returned, they found Kayla and Sam huddled by the fire, their faces lit by the dim, flickering light.

"You guys took forever," Kayla said, trying to keep her tone casual, though her eyes betrayed her fear. "Find anything?"

Jason shook his head. "Nothing. Just an empty room and a door that slammed shut. Probably the wind."

Sam didn't look convinced. She glanced toward the hallway, her eyes narrowing. "I don't know, you guys. This place gives me the creeps. I say we just stick together and wait until morning."

Mia nodded in agreement, her hands still trembling slightly as she took a seat by the fire. She pulled her blanket tighter around her shoulders, staring into the flickering flames. The wind outside continued to howl, a constant reminder of how isolated they were.

"It's probably just the storm," Jason said again, though even he sounded unsure now. "Everything sounds scarier when it's dark and cold. Let's just chill until the power comes back on."

Kayla shook her head, her eyes narrowing at Jason. "If it comes back on."

The room fell silent again, each of them lost in their own thoughts. Mia couldn't shake the image of that shadow in the hallway. Her heart pounded in her chest, each beat echoing in her ears. A cold sweat formed on her skin, and her hands trembled slightly, the fear gripping her like a vice. She kept telling herself it was nothing, that it was just her mind playing tricks on her, but a part of her couldn't let it go.

Suddenly, there was another noise—a soft thud, followed by a faint scratching sound, like nails scraping against wood. Jason tightened his grip on the flashlight, his knuckles whitening. Mia and Tyler exchanged nervous glances, their breaths catching as they listened, the fear palpable between them. Everyone froze, their eyes widening as they glanced toward the door.

"There it is again," Tyler whispered, his face pale. "Tell me you all heard that."

Kayla clenched her jaw, her eyes darting around the room. "Okay, I've had enough of this. Someone is messing with us."

Jason sighed, rubbing a hand over his face. "There's no one here but us, Kayla. I don't know what's going on, but—"

Before he could finish, the scratching grew louder, more insistent. It sounded like it was coming from just outside the door, something—or someone—trying to get in. Jason felt a shiver run down his spine, his body tensing involuntarily. Mia clutched Tyler's arm, her eyes wide with fear, and Tyler's breath came out in shaky puffs as they all stared at the door.. Sam let out a nervous laugh, though it sounded forced. "Maybe it's just an animal. Like a raccoon or something."

"In this weather?" Mia asked, her voice cracking slightly. "No way."

The sound stopped abruptly, leaving an eerie silence in its wake. Everyone held their breath, waiting, listening. The wind outside seemed to howl louder, as if mocking them.

"We need to stay calm," Jason said, his voice barely above a whisper. "If it's someone messing with us, they want us to freak out. Let's just stay together, keep the fire going, and wait for morning."

Mia nodded, though her eyes remained fixed on the door, her heart pounding in her chest. She couldn't shake the feeling that something was out there—something that wanted them to be scared, to feel trapped.

Sam leaned over, her flashlight flickering as she adjusted it.

"Maybe we should just barricade the door, just in case. You know, to be safe."

Kayla nodded quickly, her face pale. "Yeah, I'm all for that."

They worked together, moving a heavy piece of furniture in front of the door. It wasn't much, but it made them feel a little safer, as if they had some control over the situation. Once the door was barricaded, they all sat back down, the fire crackling softly in the otherwise silent room.

Mia glanced at her phone, the screen still showing no signal. She sighed, leaning her head back against the couch. "This is not how I imagined this trip going."

Tyler let out a nervous laugh. "Yeah, I was hoping for hot chocolate and movie marathons, not... whatever this is."

Jason forced a smile, though it didn't reach his eyes. Inside, he felt a gnawing sense of unease, a voice in the back of his mind whispering that everything wasn't as simple as he was trying to make it seem. "Hey, at least we'll have a cool story to tell when we get back, right?"

"If we get back," Kayla muttered, her eyes flicking toward the barricaded door.

Silence settled over them once again, the only sound the crackling of the fire and the relentless howling of the wind outside. Mia closed her eyes, trying to calm her racing thoughts. She kept telling herself that everything was fine, that they were just letting their imaginations get the best of them. But deep down, she knew that something was wrong—something they couldn't explain.

Hours passed, and the tension in the room seemed to ease slightly. Mia let herself relax, if only a little, trying to convince herself that they were finally safe. She glanced at the others, noticing how their tired faces softened as the fear ebbed away. Maybe they really could make it through the night, she thought, her heartbeat slowing as the silence settled comfortably around them. They took turns keeping watch, the others dozing off in fits and starts. The wind outside had died down a bit, and the scratching at the door had stopped. For a brief moment, Mia allowed herself to believe that maybe, just maybe, they'd make it through the night without any more scares.

But then, just as the first light of dawn began to filter through the snow-covered windows, bringing with it a sudden chill that seemed out of place. Mia opened her eyes and saw it—a shadow, standing at the far end of the hallway, watching them. She blinked, her breath catching in her throat, her heart pounding in her ears. The figure was tall, its form indistinct, but there was no mistaking it. A strange, faint smell of damp earth seemed to drift in, heightening the sense of unease.

She gasped, sitting up quickly, her heart pounding as adrenaline surged through her veins, fumbling for her flashlight. "Guys," she whispered, her voice trembling. "Wake up."

The others stirred, groggy and confused. Jason rubbed his eyes, blinking at her. "What is it, Mia?"

Mia pointed toward the hallway, her hand shaking. "There's someone... there's something there."

Jason turned, his eyes narrowing as he shone his flashlight down the hallway. But there was nothing—just shadows cast by the rising sun. He looked back at Mia, his expression a mix of concern and confusion. "I don't see anything."

Mia's heart pounded, her eyes still fixed on the hallway. She knew what she had seen. She wasn't imagining it. Something was there —something that wanted them to be afraid.

And somehow, she knew this was only the beginning.

CHAPTER 3: THE LEGEND OF KRAMPUS

The next morning came with a crisp chill, the remnants of the previous night's unease still hanging heavily in the lodge. The sky outside was overcast, the snow piling up even higher against the windows. Jason was the first one awake, rubbing the sleep from his eyes as he started a fire to warm up the living room. The initial chill of the room clung to him, and the crackling of the fire gradually filled the silence, bringing a sense of comfort. One by one, the others groggily joined him, drawn by the warmth and the faint crackling of the newly kindled flames.

"Morning," Mia muttered as she wrapped a blanket around her shoulders and sat down by the fire. Her gaze shifted over to Jason, who had his eyes glued to his phone. "Any signal yet?"

Jason shook his head. "Nah. Still nothing. We're cut off until the storm clears, I guess." He threw another log onto the fire, sighing as he stared into the flames. "Guess we're roughing it for real."

Kayla yawned as she walked into the room, clutching a mug of steaming coffee. A sense of unease clung to her, her eyes darting nervously to the shadows as if expecting something to emerge. "I hate this place. It's so creepy, and I didn't sleep at all last night," she complained, dropping onto the couch beside Mia.

"Did you hear those noises again?" Sam asked, joining the group. Her face was drawn, her eyes heavy with dark circles, like she hadn't rested well either.

"I tried not to listen," Kayla replied, shaking her head. "I figured it was just the wind or my imagination."

Tyler, who had been rummaging through some old cupboards, called out from the corner of the room, his voice filled with excitement and curiosity. "Hey, check this out!" He held up an old, dust-covered book, its spine cracked and the pages yellowed with age.

Mia frowned, squinting at it. "What is that?"

"Found it in the library over there," Tyler said, pointing to a small, tucked-away room they hadn't noticed the day before. "Thought it might be interesting."

"Yeah, because dusty old books are really what we need right now," Kayla said sarcastically, but Tyler ignored her, already flipping through the pages.

"Whoa, guys, listen to this," Tyler said, his voice dropping a notch, taking on a more serious tone. The others turned their attention toward him as he began to read aloud. "The Legend of Krampus—a towering, horned creature with glowing red eyes and sharp claws, who visits those who have been naughty, punishing them for their wrongdoings. His twisted, goat-like features and the clanging of heavy chains strike fear into anyone who hears him approach."

Mia raised an eyebrow. "Krampus? Isn't that like... an old Christmas story?"

Tyler nodded. "Yeah, kind of. It's like the opposite of Santa. Instead of bringing presents to the good kids, Krampus comes for the bad ones. But this story..." He paused, his eyes scanning the page. "It says that children went missing around Christmas, years ago, in this very region. They say Krampus would come to collect them."

Kayla shivered, leaning back against the couch. She rubbed her arms, trying to ward off the cold that seemed to seep into her bones, but it wasn't just the chill—there was something about the story that had gotten under her skin, a gnawing sense of dread she couldn't shake. "Okay, that's officially the creepiest thing I've heard in a while."

Jason shook his head, letting out a nervous laugh. "It's just some folklore, guys. Come on, every town has some spooky ghost story or whatever." He rolled his eyes, but his smile faltered slightly, as if trying to convince himself. He paused, his smile faltering slightly, as if trying to convince himself. "It's probably all made up to scare kids into behaving."

"Maybe," Tyler said, though his eyes remained on the page, his voice betraying a hint of doubt. "But it's weird how specific this is. It even mentions symbols that were used to keep Krampus away."

Sam leaned forward, intrigued. "What kind of symbols?"

Tyler turned the book around, showing them a page filled with hand-drawn sketches of strange symbols, each one more intricate than the last. "These," he said, pointing at a circular design. "Supposedly, they were carved around homes to protect people from Krampus."

Mia frowned, her gaze lingering on the symbols. "So, what happens if you don't have these symbols?"

Tyler shrugged. "According to the story, Krampus comes for you."

The room fell silent, the crackling of the fire the only sound breaking the tension. Kayla rolled her eyes, trying to brush off the growing discomfort. "Yeah, well, I'm pretty sure we'll be fine without a bunch of ancient doodles." She picked up her phone, refreshing it uselessly. "I just wish the signal would come back."

"Yeah, well, don't say I didn't warn you," Tyler said, closing the book but still eyeing it with a hint of unease.

Later that day, as the group busied themselves trying to pass the time—playing card games and sharing snacks—Jason stumbled across something. A faint scratching sound caught his attention, making him pause. As he ran his fingers over the back of the lodge's heavy wooden door, he felt the rough texture of something etched into the surface. It made his blood run cold. Scratched into the back of the lodge's heavy wooden door was a symbol. The jagged lines seemed to pulse with an unsettling energy, the edges rough under Jason's fingertips. A sense of dread settled over him as he traced the design, his stomach churning as if something dark was lurking just beyond sight. It was faint, barely visible under the layers of dust and grime, but unmistakable. It was the same symbol Tyler had shown them from the book.

"Uh, guys?" Jason called out, his voice wavering slightly. The others gathered around, their expressions a mix of confusion and concern.

"Is that..." Mia started, her voice trailing off as she exchanged a glance with Tyler.

"It's one of the symbols," Tyler confirmed, swallowing hard. "The protection symbols from the book. But why would it be here?"

"Maybe someone else believed in the story," Sam suggested, her voice uneasy. "Maybe they thought it would protect them."

Kayla shook her head. "Yeah, well, it doesn't seem like it worked if they're not here anymore, does it?"

"We don't know that," Tyler countered. "Maybe it did work, and that's why they're gone—they left, they survived."

The uneasy feeling in the pit of Mia's stomach grew stronger. She rubbed her arms, trying to shake off the chill that had settled there. "Can we just not talk about this anymore? It's really starting to freak me out."

"Agreed," Jason said, stepping away from the door. "Let's just... let's just focus on getting through today. Hopefully, the storm will let up soon."

As the afternoon turned into evening, the group tried to distract themselves with board games and snacks. Sam attempted to lighten the mood by making jokes, but the atmosphere remained tense, the strange symbol lurking at the back of all their minds.

At one point, Sam glanced around the room, a mischievous grin forming on her face. "So, do you think we're on Krampus's naughty list? I mean, we're stuck here, cut off from everything—kind of feels like punishment."

Tyler groaned. "Really, Sam? That's not helping."

"Hey, just trying to make light of the situation," Sam said with a shrug. "Besides, if Krampus does show up, I'd like to know which one of you guys got us into this mess."

Kayla rolled her eyes. "It was probably you."

Their laughter, though forced, was short-lived. As the sun began to set, strange new sights started appearing around the lodge. Jason was the first to notice—the symbols, similar to the one on the door, were now scratched into different pieces of furniture. One on the back of an old chair, another carved faintly into the frame of the window.

"Uh, guys," Jason called, his voice shaky. "I think we have a problem."

Mia turned toward him, her stomach dropping as she saw the expression on his face. "What is it now?"

Jason pointed at the back of the chair, the scratched symbol clearly visible in the dim light. Tyler came over, his eyes widening as he saw it. "Okay, that's definitely not good."

Kayla frowned, her eyes darting between the various symbols. "Is someone trying to mess with us? Who would even do that?"

"No one else is here," Mia said, her voice trembling. "It has to be... something else."

The atmosphere shifted, growing heavy with tension as they each stared at the symbols. The wind outside picked up again, howling through the cracks in the windows, almost as if it was trying to get inside.

"Okay, everyone just calm down," Jason said, trying to keep his voice steady, though a nervous chuckle escaped his lips. He fidgeted with his sleeve, glancing over his shoulder as if to reassure himself. "We don't know what's going on, but freaking out isn't going to help. We just need to stick together, stay by the fire, and not wander off."

Tyler nodded, though he couldn't seem to tear his eyes away from the symbols. His breathing grew shallow, and his hands clenched at his sides, the unease settling in deeper as he tried to make sense of what he was seeing. "We need to figure out what these mean— why they're here."

"We already know why," Kayla snapped. "It's Krampus, isn't it? The book said the symbols were supposed to keep him away, but they're everywhere. Maybe they're not working."

Mia hugged her knees to her chest, her heart pounding. Her voice broke slightly as she spoke, her eyes welling up. "I don't want to believe in any of this. I just want to go home."

"We all do," Jason said softly, moving closer to her. "We're going to be okay. It's just a storm, and it's just an old story. Nothing's going to happen."

But as the night closed in around them, and the wind outside turned into an almost human-like wail, the group couldn't shake the feeling that something was indeed very, very wrong. The symbols were multiplying, appearing in places they hadn't seen before, almost as if they were being carved while the group wasn't looking. Mia felt a knot tighten in her stomach, a deep sense of fear creeping in as she watched the symbols appear, her mind racing with dark possibilities.

They huddled together by the fire, the room filled with the flickering orange light, the symbols casting dark, twisted shadows on the walls. Tyler kept the old book in his lap, flipping through the pages, hoping to find something—anything—that might explain what was happening, some way to stop it.

But the more he read, the more hopeless it seemed. Each new line filled him with a growing sense of dread, the realization sinking in that there might be no way out. His hands trembled slightly as he turned the pages, his mind grappling with the fear that they were truly trapped. The story wasn't just some old folklore—it was a warning, and it felt like they were living it. The lines between the legend and their reality blurred, and as the night grew darker, they couldn't help but wonder if Krampus was already here, watching, waiting for the right moment to strike. A sudden rustle echoed from the shadows, followed by the flicker of a shadow across the wall, making their hearts pound in unison.

CHAPTER 4: VANISHING FOOTSTEPS

When Mia woke up, her head fuzzy with sleep, it was still dark. She blinked, the flickering embers from the fire providing the only light in the room. She glanced around, something feeling... off. Jason was curled up under a blanket near the hearth, Kayla sprawled out on the couch, and Sam was curled in an armchair, her face half-buried under a scarf. But Tyler's spot, near the far side of the room, was empty.

Mia rubbed her eyes, sitting up straighter. She squinted, trying to make out his shape in the dim light. Nothing. A sense of unease started to settle in her chest, her mind racing with possibilities. His blanket was a crumpled heap, and his boots, which had been next to the fireplace to dry, were gone.

"Jason," she whispered, nudging him with her foot. "Jason, wake up."

Jason groaned, pushing the blanket away from his face and blinking blearily up at her. "What is it?" he mumbled.

"Tyler's gone," Mia said, her voice trembling slightly.

Jason pushed himself up onto his elbows, glancing at the empty spot where Tyler had been. "Maybe he just went to the bathroom or something," he muttered, though his voice lacked conviction. He sighed, his eyes flicking nervously toward the dark hallway before returning to Mia. He pulled out his phone, but the screen was dark—still no signal.

"Then why would he take his boots?" Mia asked, her eyes darting to the window, where the snow was still falling heavily.

Kayla stirred at the noise, her eyes fluttering open. "What's going on?" she asked, her voice groggy.

"Tyler's missing," Mia repeated, the words feeling heavier each time she said them. "And it's still storming."

Sam woke up next, rubbing her eyes as she sat up, looking around. "Wait, what do you mean he's missing? He was right here."

"Well, he's not now," Jason said, pushing himself to his feet. He walked over to the window, peering outside. The world was a swirling mass of white, the wind howling across the snow-covered landscape. He turned back to the group, his face tense. "We need to find him."

"In this?" Kayla asked, her eyes wide with disbelief. "Are you serious? He could be anywhere."

"He could be in trouble," Mia shot back, her voice shaking. "We can't just sit here and do nothing."

Jason nodded, his jaw set, already pulling on his coat and gloves. His eyes were determined, but his hands shook slightly as he tugged at the fabric, his movements quick, almost frantic. "Mia's right. We can't just leave him out there. Kayla, Sam, you guys stay here and keep the fire going. We'll be back as soon as we can."

Kayla looked like she wanted to argue, but she glanced at the swirling snow outside and bit her lip, nodding reluctantly. "Just... be careful, okay?"

Mia pulled on her coat, the cold hitting her immediately as Jason opened the door. The wind whipped through the room, and she shivered, pulling her scarf up over her nose. Jason gave her a reassuring nod, and together, they stepped out into the storm.

The snow was deep, their boots sinking in with each step as they made their way away from the lodge. The crunch of the snow underfoot was nearly drowned out by the howling wind, and the cold seemed to seep through their layers, biting at their skin. The wind was relentless, biting through their layers and making it hard to see more than a few feet ahead. Jason held up his flashlight, the beam barely cutting through the swirling snow.

"Tyler!" he called out, his voice barely audible over the howling wind. "Tyler, where are you?!"

Mia joined in, her voice cracking from the cold. "Tyler! If you can hear us, say something!"

They trudged forward, their breaths visible in the frigid air. The snow crunched under their feet, the sound almost swallowed by the storm. Mia's breath hitched in her throat, her vision swimming slightly with dizziness. Her hands trembled uncontrollably inside her gloves as they moved further away from the lodge. What if Tyler was hurt? What if he was lost? What if...

"Look!" Jason suddenly shouted, pointing ahead. Mia squinted, her eyes straining against the wind. In the dim light, she could just make out a line of footprints, half-buried in the fresh snow. Relief flooded through her as she realized they were Tyler's. They led away from the lodge, toward the tree line. But as they approached, her relief quickly shifted to dread. There was something else— another set of tracks, larger, with deep, pointed impressions.

"What the..." Jason muttered, crouching down to examine the prints. They were hoof-like, the shape unmistakable even in the dim light. Mia's stomach twisted, the unease from the previous days returning in full force. She thought back to the strange noises in the night, the feeling of being watched, and the symbols that seemed to appear out of nowhere, all of it piling on her nerves, making her feel like something terrible was closing in.

"Do you think..." she started, her voice trailing off, the words catching in her throat. She didn't want to say it, didn't want to give form to the fear that had been growing inside her.

Jason stood, his face pale. "I don't know. But we need to find Tyler. Now."

They followed the footprints, the trees closing in around them as they moved deeper into the woods. The branches creaked above them, weighed down by the heavy snow, and the wind howled through the gaps, creating an eerie, almost mournful sound. The cold stung their faces, seeping through their clothes and biting at their skin. Their fingers felt numb, and the wind roared in their ears, the snow soaking through their clothes and blurring their vision, making every step feel like a struggle against the elements. Mia's flashlight flickered, and she tapped it nervously, her chest tightening, her hands feeling clammy.

"Tyler!" she called again, her voice echoing through the trees. "Please, answer us!"

Jason held up a hand, stopping her. He pointed ahead, and Mia's heart skipped a beat. Half-buried in the snow was Tyler's phone, the screen cracked, the case covered in frost. Mia rushed forward, picking it up, her hands trembling.

"This is his," she whispered, her breath visible in the cold air. She turned to Jason, her eyes wide with fear. "What happened to him?"

Jason didn't answer, his eyes scanning the darkness around them. The hoof-like prints continued further into the woods, and Mia's stomach twisted painfully. She felt tears prick at her eyes, the cold stinging her face as she tried to blink them away.

"We have to keep going," Jason said, his voice grim. He turned, following the tracks, and Mia took a deep breath, steeling herself before following him.

The further they went, the darker it seemed to get. The trees closed in around them, their branches like skeletal fingers reaching down, and the wind seemed to carry whispers, barely audible over the howling. Mia's flashlight flickered again, the beam sputtering before going out completely.

"Jason, wait," she called, her voice shaking as she struggled to get her flashlight working again. Jason turned back, his own light barely illuminating his face.

"We can't stop, Mia," he said, his voice urgent. "We have to find him."

Mia nodded, though fear was clawing at her insides. A chill ran down her spine, her skin prickling as she couldn't shake the feeling that something terrible was watching them, waiting for the right moment. She fumbled with her flashlight, finally getting it to flicker back to life. She looked up, and her breath caught in her throat. In the dim light, just beyond Jason, she saw something—a shadow, tall and hunched, moving between the trees.

"Jason!" she screamed, her voice breaking. Jason spun around, his flashlight beam cutting through the darkness, but there was nothing there. The shadow was gone.

"What? What is it?" Jason asked, his eyes wide.

Mia shook her head, her heart pounding, her hands trembling. "I... I saw something. It was right there.""

Jason's face hardened, his jaw clenching as he took a step toward her, his shoulders stiffening, his eyes scanning the darkness. "We need to get back to the lodge. Now."

Mia opened her mouth to argue, but the fear in Jason's eyes silenced her. She nodded, and they turned, following their own footsteps back through the snow. The oppressive silence between them seemed to amplify the urgency, the wind howling around them as if urging them to move faster. The wind seemed to howl louder, the cold biting at their skin, and Mia's heart raced as they hurried through the woods, the shadows seeming to move just beyond the edge of their lights.

When they finally stumbled back into the lodge, the door slamming shut behind them, Mia collapsed onto the floor, her hands trembling. The sudden warmth of the lodge enveloped her, a stark contrast to the freezing cold outside, offering a fleeting sense of relief despite her exhaustion. Kayla and Sam rushed over, their faces pale, their eyes wide with fear.

"Did you find him?" Kayla asked, her voice barely above a whisper.

Mia shook her head, tears spilling down her cheeks. She held up Tyler's phone, her voice breaking. "We found this... but no sign of him."

The room fell silent, the fire crackling in the hearth the only sound. Jason sank into a chair, his face buried in his hands. "We have to figure out what's going on," he said, his voice muffled. "We can't just sit here and wait for whatever this is to come for us next."

Kayla glanced at the window, the storm still raging outside. Her voice dropped to a whisper, and her eyes darted to the shadows. "You think it's... you think it's him, don't you? The thing from the book. Krampus." The group exchanged nervous glances, a heavy silence settling over them, each of them shivering slightly as the implication sank in."

No one answered, but the fear in their eyes was enough. Mia hugged her knees to her chest, her chest tightening, her breath catching as her mind raced. Whatever was out there, it had Tyler. And if they didn't figure out how to stop it, they might all be next.

CHAPTER 5: THE HUNTER REVEALED

Back at the lodge, the fire had dwindled down to a mere glow, casting flickering shadows across the walls. The lingering warmth of the dying fire mixed with the faint smell of smoke, adding a fleeting sense of comfort to the otherwise tense atmosphere. Kayla and Sam sat close to the fireplace, the uneasy silence between them only broken by the occasional crackle of the embers. Kayla chewed on her lower lip, her gaze shifting nervously from the darkened windows to the fireplace, as if expecting Krampus to emerge from the shadows. She couldn't shake the feeling that something might be lurking there, hidden just beyond the reach of the dying fire's glow. Her mind filled with images of shadowy figures, silent and patient, waiting for the perfect moment to strike.

Jason and Mia had left hours earlier for one last time, determined to find Tyler after he had vanished without a trace. They had found another clue—Tyler's scarf caught on a branch near the edge of the woods, flapping in the wind. Desperation drove them; they couldn't just sit back and do nothing while their friend was out there. Despite the storm, they held onto a fragile hope that maybe, just maybe, they could bring him back. They couldn't just sit and do nothing, even though the storm raged outside, making any search dangerous. Kayla felt a mix of anger and fear. Anger because she knew splitting up was risky. Fear because deep down, she wondered if they'd ever come back. Her stomach churned, and her hands balled into fists, trying to suppress the unease gnawing at her. It was the not knowing that gnawed at her, the helplessness of waiting while their friends faced whatever was out there.

"I can't take this," she finally said, her voice barely above a whisper. "Why did they have to go again? We should have all stayed together."

Sam shook her head, rubbing her temples. "They had to, Kayla. We couldn't just leave Tyler out there alone. But this place..." She paused, her eyes scanning the room. "This place feels wrong. I swear I keep hearing things."

Kayla opened her mouth to respond, but before she could, a noise echoed through the lodge—a low, groaning sound, almost like a door creaking open. Their breaths caught, muscles tensing as they instinctively shrank back, fear gripping them. They both froze, their eyes wide as they turned toward the direction of the noise. It came from the basement.

"Did you hear that?" Sam whispered, her voice trembling.

Kayla nodded, her face pale. "Yeah. And I really wish I hadn't."

They exchanged a look, the fear mirrored in each other's eyes. Sam took a deep breath, standing up slowly. Her eyes were wide, her jaw clenched as she fought to steady her trembling hands. Her breath hitched, and her knees felt weak, but she forced herself to move, trying to push past the fear. "We need to check it out. We can't just ignore it. What if... what if it's Tyler?"

Kayla swallowed hard, her hands shaking as she pushed herself to her feet. Cold sweat coated her palms, and her chest tightened with each shaky breath, fear clawing at her insides. "Fine. But if it's something else, I'm blaming you for this."

They grabbed their phones, turning on their flashlights as they made their way to the basement door. The air seemed colder as they approached. Their breaths grew shallow, and a shiver ran down their spines. With each step, the feeling of dread grew heavier. The door stood slightly ajar, a sliver of darkness visible through the gap.

Sam reached out, her hand trembling as she pushed the door open further. It creaked loudly, the sound echoing through the otherwise silent lodge. She swallowed, glancing back at Kayla before starting down the stairs.

"Be careful," Kayla whispered, her voice barely audible over the pounding of her heart.

The stairs creaked under their weight, each step taking them deeper into the dark, musty basement. The air seemed thicker, damp with the smell of mold and mildew, making it hard to breathe and adding to the oppressive feeling that surrounded them. Sam held her phone up, the flashlight beam sweeping across the cluttered space—old furniture, dusty boxes, cobwebs hanging from the ceiling.

Suddenly, there was a noise—a rustling sound from the far corner of the basement, like something brushing against the wall, a deliberate movement that made their skin crawl. Sam froze, her breath catching in her throat as she turned the flashlight in the direction of the sound. Her mind raced with dread, imagining the worst—something monstrous lurking just out of sight, ready to pounce. The beam flickered slightly, and for a split second, she saw it—a silhouette, massive and hunched, with large horns curving up toward the ceiling. Its eyes glowed, reflecting the light from her phone, and an aura of pure malice seemed to radiate from its form.

Kayla let out a scream, the sound piercing the heavy silence, making everything feel more immediate and chaotic. Her knees buckled, and her vision blurred from panic as she struggled to stay upright. The sudden noise seemed to shatter their fragile composure, their fear surging as the oppressive quiet was violently broken. The creature moved, shifting in the shadows, and Sam grabbed Kayla's arm, pulling her back up the stairs. They stumbled, nearly falling in their haste as they scrambled to get away, their legs feeling weak and unsteady, their vision blurring from the adrenaline and panic. The door slammed shut behind them as they burst into the living room, their breaths coming in ragged gasps.

"What was that?!" Kayla cried, her voice shaking as she leaned against the door, her hands trembling.

Sam shook her head, her eyes wide with fear. "I don't know. I don't know, but it's real. It's here."

They quickly moved to barricade the door, pushing a heavy cabinet in front of it. The cabinet was heavy, its weight straining their already tired muscles, and it took all their effort to inch it across the floor, their urgency fueling every strained movement. Kayla's hands were still shaking, her heart pounding so hard she thought it might burst out of her chest. They collapsed onto the couch, their eyes fixed on the door, waiting, listening for any sign that the creature was coming after them.

"We need to get out of here," Kayla whispered, her voice breaking. "We can't stay here."

"We can't leave," Sam replied, her eyes still on the door. "Not without the others. We have to wait for Jason and Mia."

Minutes felt like hours as they sat there, the silence of the lodge broken only by the howling wind outside. Every creak, every groan of the old building made them jump, their eyes darting to the barricaded door. Kayla hugged her knees to her chest, her mind racing with thoughts of what they had seen—those glowing eyes, the horns, the darkness that seemed to seep from its very being. She could still feel the oppressive presence of the creature in the basement, its malevolence lingering like a shadow, suffocating and cold. She could still feel the coldness of its gaze, an oppressive chill that seemed to pierce right through her, making her shiver.

Finally, there was a knock on the door. It was Mia and Jason. They stumbled inside, their faces flushed from the cold, their eyes wide with fear. Kayla and Sam's heads snapped up, a mix of relief and lingering panic washing over them. Sam let out a shaky breath, her shoulders relaxing slightly, while Kayla felt her heart slow, the immediate tension easing for just a moment. Kayla and Sam's heads snapped up, a mix of relief and lingering panic washing over them. For a moment, the tension eased, but the chaos of the situation still clung to the air, keeping their nerves on edge. They slammed the door shut behind them, leaning against it as they tried to catch their breath.

"What happened?" Jason asked, his eyes moving from Kayla to Sam, noticing the barricade in front of the basement door.

Kayla shook her head, tears welling in her eyes. "There's something down there, Jason. We saw it. It's real." Jason's face shifted, a mix of skepticism and fear crossing his features. He opened his mouth, then closed it, as if struggling to decide whether to believe them or dismiss it as hysteria."

Mia's face went pale, her eyes widening. "What do you mean? What did you see?"

Sam took a deep breath, her voice trembling as she spoke. "It had horns, glowing eyes. It was... it was like the thing from the book. The Krampus."

Jason exchanged a look with Mia, his face grim. No sign of Tyler. And there were... tracks. Not human."

Mia nodded, her voice barely above a whisper. "We think it's hunting us. Whatever it is, it's not human." Kayla shivered, her eyes flicking nervously to the window, as if expecting to see something staring back at her. Sam swallowed hard, her body tensing at the realization of what they were facing."

The room fell silent, the weight of their situation settling over them like a heavy blanket. The wind howled outside, and the lodge creaked under the strain, emphasizing the stillness and tension that hung in the air. They were trapped, cut off from the world by the storm, and something was out there—something that wanted them. Mia hugged her arms around herself, her eyes darting to the windows, the shadows outside seeming to shift and move in the dim light.

"We need a plan," Jason finally said, his voice steady despite the fear in his eyes. "We can't just sit here and wait for it to pick us off one by one. We need to figure out how to fight it."

Sam nodded, though her hands were still trembling. "The book mentioned symbols. Protection symbols. Maybe... maybe we can use them."

Kayla frowned, her eyes narrowing. "You really think some old symbols are going to stop that thing? We need something real—something that can actually hurt it."

"We don't have much of a choice," Mia said, her voice firm. "We use whatever we can. We have to try."

Jason nodded, his eyes meeting each of theirs in turn. "We stick together, we don't split up, and we do whatever it takes to survive. We're not letting this thing win."

The group moved closer to the fire, their fear momentarily replaced by determination. Jason clenched his fists, his jaw tightening, while Kayla straightened her posture, her eyes hardening with resolve. They knew the odds were against them, but they had each other, and they weren't going down without a fight.

CHAPTER 6: A TOWN'S DARK SECRET

The storm had not let up since Jason and Mia returned, the wind hammering against the lodge. The group sat by the dying fire, exchanging fearful glances as the weight of their situation pressed down on them. Whatever was hunting them wasn't just a story; it was real, and it wouldn't stop until it got what it wanted.

Mia stared at the flickering flames, her mind racing for any clue, any hint that might help them. She thought back to the day they first arrived in the town, remembering the unsettling silence of the streets, the way the townspeople had avoided eye contact, as if they knew something she didn't. She recalled the whispers she had overheard in the general store about 'outsiders' and 'keeping it satisfied.' All these fragments seemed meaningless at the time, but now they tugged at her, forming pieces of a puzzle she desperately needed to solve.

Then, suddenly, she remembered something—something she had seen when they first arrived in the town. It was the old chapel, partially hidden by the overgrown trees, with strange symbols carved into the stone above the entrance. At the time, it had seemed like just another abandoned building, but now it stood out in her memory, nagging at her. She turned to Jason, her eyes wide. "The chapel," she said, her voice urgent. "When we drove in, I saw a small chapel on the edge of town. Maybe there's something there —some kind of record, a clue that might tell us how to stop this."

Jason frowned, considering her words. He glanced at the storm raging outside, his brow furrowing in concern. "A chapel? Are you sure it's worth it? We don't know what we're dealing with, and going out in this storm is dangerous.""

"But we can't just stay here and wait," Mia replied, her voice trembling. "We need answers, Jason. If there's any chance of finding something, anything, that can help us, we have to try."

Sam nodded, her expression serious. "She's right. If this thing is part of some kind of town legend, there might be something at the chapel. It's better than sitting here doing nothing."

Kayla hesitated, fear written all over her face. She couldn't shake the image of those glowing eyes and the suffocating darkness that seemed to follow them. The wind carried a faint, eerie whisper, almost like a distant voice calling her name, and the air was thick with the metallic scent of fear, making her stomach turn. "But what if we run into... it... again? We're risking our lives going out there.""

Jason took a deep breath, meeting Kayla's eyes. "We're risking our lives either way. I'd rather be doing something to help us get out of this." He turned back to Mia, determination in his eyes. "Okay, let's do it. But we stick together. We go to the chapel, and we come right back. No splitting up, no wandering off."

With a plan decided, they gathered whatever supplies they could find—flashlights, extra coats, and the old book Tyler had found, in case it contained any useful information. They wrapped themselves in scarves and gloves, bracing themselves for the storm, before stepping outside into the howling wind.

The cold hit them like a wall as they pushed forward, their flashlights barely piercing the blinding white. Their fingers grew numb despite their gloves, and the howling wind swallowed all other sounds. They moved in a tight group, Jason leading the way, Mia right behind him, followed closely by Sam and Kayla. The world around them was a blur of snow and darkness, the wind carrying strange sounds—whispers, like voices just out of reach—that made their skin crawl.

"Keep moving!" Jason shouted over the roar of the storm, his voice barely audible. They trudged forward, each step feeling like a battle as the snow threatened to pull them under. Mia's heart pounded in her chest, fear and cold gnawing at her resolve. She kept her eyes on Jason's back, focusing on his steady movements to keep herself calm.

Finally, after what felt like an eternity, the outline of the chapel came into view—a small, dark shape against the swirling snow. Relief washed over Mia, her shoulders loosening as she let out a deep breath, giving her the strength to push forward. They reached the chapel door, and Jason shoved it open, the old wood creaking loudly as they stumbled inside, out of the biting wind.

The interior of the chapel was dark and cold, the air thick with the scent of dust and old wood. Mia shivered involuntarily, her breath visible in the frigid air. A sense of foreboding settled over them, the silence pressing against her chest, making her feel as though the walls were closing in. Mia swept her flashlight across the room, revealing rows of worn pews and a small altar at the front. The place felt abandoned, forgotten by time, but there was a sense of something else—something that made her shiver, a presence lingering in the shadows. She couldn't shake the feeling that the very walls were watching, that the spirit they had heard about might be lurking here, unseen but aware of their every move.

"Is anyone here?" Jason called out, his voice echoing through the empty space. For a moment, there was only silence, the wind howling outside the only sound. Then, a rustling came from the far corner, and they all turned, their flashlights converging on the source.

An old woman stepped out from the shadows, her face lined with age, her eyes hollow. The group gasped, instinctively stepping back, their eyes widening in shock at her sudden appearance. She wore a thick shawl, her hands trembling slightly as she raised them in greeting. The group gasped, instinctively stepping back, their eyes widening in shock at her sudden appearance. "You shouldn't be here," she said, her voice raspy, almost lost in the sound of the storm outside.

Mia took a step forward, her heart pounding. She felt the desperation rising in her chest, the fear of what might happen if they couldn't find a way out. "Please, we need your help. There's something out there—something hunting us. We don't know what it is or how to stop it."

The old woman stared at them for a long moment, her eyes narrowing. Then she nodded slowly, her movements deliberate, almost reluctant, motioning for them to come closer. Her voice, barely above a whisper, seemed to struggle against the howling storm outside. "You're not the first to come looking for answers," she said, her voice barely above a whisper. "This town... it carries a dark burden. A burden we brought upon ourselves."

Jason exchanged a wary glance with Mia before stepping forward. "What do you mean? What burden?"

The old woman sighed, her gaze distant. "Years ago, when times were hard, the townspeople made a pact—a deal to protect themselves from the harsh winters, from famine, from suffering." They called upon an ancient force, a dark spirit, and promised it a sacrifice in exchange for its protection."

The group exchanged nervous glances, Kayla's breath catching as she instinctively stepped closer to Sam. "The spirit was Krampus —a creature that fed on fear, on the 'naughty,' those deemed unworthy. At first, it took only the children—the ones who misbehaved, who broke the rules. But over time, the pact grew darker, the sacrifices greater. Outsiders, travelers, anyone who stumbled upon our town became fair game. It was the only way to keep the creature satisfied, to keep it from turning on us."

Kayla gasped, her face pale, taking a step back, her entire body trembling. "You sacrificed people? To that... thing?"

The woman nodded, her eyes haunted. "We had no choice. It was either them or us. And now, you are here. You've seen it, haven't you? It knows you are here, and it will not stop until it has what it wants."

A heavy silence fell over the group, the weight of the woman's words sinking in. Mia felt her knees weaken, her mind racing. They had walked straight into a trap—a town cursed by its own dark past, a creature that wouldn't rest until it had claimed its due.

Jason clenched his jaw, his face hardening with determination. He thought of his sister, of the promise he made to himself to never let anyone else suffer because of his inaction. "There has to be a way to stop it. There has to be something we can do."

The old woman hesitated, her eyes shifting to the altar. "There is a way, but it is dangerous. The symbols—the protection symbols from the old texts—they can hold it off, but only for a time." The group exchanged hopeful glances, a flicker of optimism breaking through their fear as they listened, each of them clinging to the possibility of a way out. To truly break the pact, someone must face it. Confront it."

Sam shook her head, fear evident in her eyes. "You mean... one of us has to face that thing? Alone?" Kayla's face paled further, her eyes wide with terror, while Jason placed a reassuring hand on Sam's shoulder, his expression fierce with determination. "We'll figure it out," he said, his voice steady, trying to calm the rising panic.

The woman nodded solemnly. "It is the only way. If you can weaken it, drive it back, you might be able to escape. But it will not be easy. The creature feeds on fear—it will use your worst nightmares against you."

Mia swallowed hard, her heart pounding in her chest. Her hands trembled slightly, and a cold sweat formed on her brow. The thought of facing that thing, of standing up to it, was terrifying. But what choice did they have? They couldn't just sit back and wait to be picked off one by one. They had to fight, no matter how impossible it seemed.

Jason turned to the group, his eyes fierce. "We came here together, and we're going to get out of this together. We use the symbols, we protect ourselves, and we find a way to end this."

The old woman stepped back, her eyes filled with a mix of pity and hope. "I will help you as much as I can. But remember—Krampus is powerful, and it will not give up easily.

Mia nodded, her hands trembling as she gripped her flashlight. She looked at her friends—Jason, Sam, Kayla—and saw the same fear in their eyes, but also the same determination. Jason gave her a small nod, and Sam reached out, giving Mia's arm a reassuring squeeze. It was a silent promise—they were in this together. They had come this far, and they weren't about to back down now.

"Let's do this," Mia said, her voice steady despite the fear coursing through her. "Together."

The old woman handed them a piece of chalk, her fingers brushing against Mia's as she spoke one last time. A shiver ran down Mia's spine at the touch, an unsettling mix of fear and a strange sense of reassurance. "Mark the symbols. Protect yourselves. And remember—courage is your only weapon against the darkness."

With the storm still raging outside, they turned and left the chapel, their hearts heavy but resolute. They had a plan, however desperate it might be. The creature was hunting them, but they weren't about to go down without a fight.

CHAPTER 7: NO WAY OUT

The blizzard outside had escalated into a full-blown nightmare, with gusts of wind battering the lodge and snow piling up against the windows, threatening to bury them alive.

"Anything?" Sam asked, her eyes darting toward Mia, who had her phone raised, desperately trying to find a signal.

Mia shook her head, frustration evident on her face. "Still nothing. We're completely cut off." She threw her phone down on the couch, exhaling sharply. She could feel a tight knot forming in her chest, the helplessness gnawing at her—how could they fight what they couldn't even understand, when they couldn't even call for help?

Jason stood by the window, staring out into the endless swirl of white. The storm was relentless, showing no signs of letting up. "We have to find another way," he muttered, running a hand through his hair. "We can't just sit here and do nothing."

"Like what?" Kayla snapped, her voice cracking under the strain of fear. Her hands trembled, and she took a sharp intake of breath. "What else are we supposed to do, Jason? We're stuck here, in the middle of nowhere, with no way to contact anyone. And in case you haven't noticed, there's something out there. Something that wants us dead."

Jason turned, meeting her gaze with a determined look. "The radio," he said. "The old one in the basement. If it still works, maybe we can get a signal out—contact someone, anyone, who can help."

Kayla rolled her eyes, scoffing. She began pacing, her hands moving in frustrated gestures. "You really think that ancient piece of junk is going to save us?"

"We have to try," Jason shot back, his frustration starting to show. "Unless you have a better idea?"

Mia stepped between them, holding up her hands. "Okay, enough. We don't have time for this. Let's just try the radio. If it doesn't work, then we'll figure something else out. But standing here arguing isn't helping anyone."

Sam nodded, standing up from her spot by the fire. "Mia's right. We need to do something. Let's go check it out."

Together, they made their way to the basement door, flashlights in hand. The air was colder down there, a damp chill that seemed to seep into their bones. A faint, musty odor hung in the air, and they could hear the distant dripping of water, each drop echoing in the silence, heightening the eerie atmosphere. The stairs creaked under their weight, and every sound seemed amplified in the silence, making their hearts race even faster.

Jason led the way, his flashlight beam sweeping across the cluttered space until he found the old radio, perched on a dusty table in the corner. It looked ancient—its dials rusted, its wires tangled—but it was their only hope.

"Here goes nothing," Jason muttered, flipping a few switches. The radio crackled to life, a hiss of static filling the basement. He turned the dials, trying to find a frequency, his movements careful and deliberate.

"Come on," Mia whispered, her breath visible in the cold air. "Please work."

Suddenly, a voice broke through the static—faint and crackling, but unmistakable. "You must leave... immediately... danger..." The group's breaths caught, and they exchanged fearful glances. Mia's hand tightened around her flashlight, her knuckles turning white, as the realization of the warning sank in.

Mia's eyes widened, and she leaned closer to the radio. "Did you hear that?" she whispered, her voice trembling.

Jason turned the dial again, trying to make the signal clearer. The voice returned, this time louder, though still distorted by the static. "Get out... it's coming..."

Kayla took a step back, her face pale, the cold air biting into her skin. "Leave? How? We can't go anywhere! There's a blizzard out there!"

Sam's expression was grim. "They're warning us. But we're trapped. There's nowhere to go."

Jason tried adjusting the dials once more, but the voice vanished, replaced by nothing but static. He let out a frustrated sigh, slamming his hand against the side of the radio. "Damn it!" His mind raced with helpless thoughts—how could he protect everyone if he couldn't even get a signal? The feeling of failure gnawed at him, making his anger even more intense.

Mia stood up, her heart pounding. "We need a plan," she said, her voice firm. "We can't just sit here and wait for whatever this is to come for us. We need to protect ourselves, somehow."

Kayla shook her head, tears welling in her eyes. "This is all your fault, Jason," she said, her voice breaking. Jason felt a pang of guilt twist in his chest, the weight of responsibility pressing down on him. He knew she was right—he had brought them here, and now he had to find a way to get them out. "You wanted to come here. You thought it would be fun. Now look where we are—Tyler's gone, and we're stuck here, with some... some monster hunting us." She thought of Tyler's laughter when Jason first suggested the trip, how he had been so eager for an adventure. Now, all that was left was fear and regret."

Jason clenched his jaw, his frustration boiling over, his hands shaking slightly. "You think I wanted this, Kayla? You think any of us did? I'm trying to fix it. We're all trying to fix it."

Mia stepped between them, her eyes flashing with determination. "This isn't helping. Fighting each other isn't going to get us out of here. We need to stick together, or we're not going to survive."

41

Kayla wiped her eyes, her voice cracking. "I'm just scared. I don't know what to do."

Sam placed a hand on Kayla's shoulder. "We're all scared. But Mia's right. We have to stay together. We can't let fear tear us apart."

The tension in the room slowly began to dissipate, and Jason took a deep breath, his shoulders relaxing. "The symbols," he said, looking at the others. "The ones from the book Tyler found.

Mia nodded, her resolve hardening. She straightened her posture, her voice becoming steadier. "Then let's do it. We need to cover every door, every window." Jason gave a firm nod, stepping forward with renewed determination, while Kayla hesitated for a moment before reluctantly nodding, her fear still evident. Sam tightened her grip on the flashlight, her eyes reflecting both fear and resolve. They each knew the stakes, and despite their apprehension, they were ready to act. And remember what the old woman said. We have to be brave and face it. We can't just keep running. If we can trap it, maybe we can destroy it."

They gathered their supplies—chalk given by old women, pieces of charcoal from the fireplace, anything they could use to draw the symbols. Working quickly, they split up, marking each window, each doorway, with the protective symbols they had memorized from the book.

The storm outside continued to howl, the wind rattling the windows as if trying to force its way inside. Mia's hands trembled as she drew the symbols on the front door, her flashlight casting long shadows across the walls. She couldn't help but think about Tyler—his laughter, his optimism, and how he would always say everything would be fine. But now, fear clawed at her, the thought that the symbols might not work making her stomach twist.

What if this was all for nothing? What if they couldn't stop it? She couldn't help but think, what if this didn't work? What if the symbols failed, and whatever was out there got in? The thought made her stomach twist, fear clawing at her as she tried to steady her shaking hands.

"Do you think this will work?" Sam asked, her voice barely a whisper.

Mia took a deep breath, her eyes meeting Sam's. "I hope so. It's all we have right now."

Once they had finished marking the lodge with symbols, they gathered in the living room, rekindling the fire to fight off the growing cold. They also gathered makeshift weapons— fireplace pokers, heavy tools, anything they could use to defend themselves.They needed to rely on that courage now more than ever. They huddled together, their eyes on the flickering flames, their ears straining for any sound beyond the walls of the lodge.

Jason sat beside Mia; his expression was weary but determined. He placed a reassuring hand on Mia's shoulder. Mia felt a flicker of comfort in his touch, a sense of shared burden that made her feel just a little less alone in the overwhelming darkness. "No one goes off alone," he said, his voice low but firm. "Whatever happens, we face it together, just like the old woman said. Courage is what will keep us alive."

Mia nodded, leaning her head against his shoulder. They had done everything they could to prepare. Now, they needed to confront whatever was coming—armed with courage and the symbols they had drawn. They would not just wait; they would face the darkness head-on, hoping to end it once and for all.

CHAPTER 8: THE FINAL STAND

Mia took a deep breath, her hands trembling slightly as she clutched a kitchen knife they had found in one of the drawers. The cold weight of the metal pressed into her palm, a stark reminder of how fragile their chances were. What if this wasn't enough? The thought gnawed at her—what if they couldn't stop it, and everything they did was for nothing? The fear of failing her friends weighed heavily on her, but she knew she had to try. "We can't just sit here and wait to die," she said, her voice cracking but determined. "If this thing wants a fight, we give it one. We make a stand. We take control."

Jason nodded, his eyes meeting each of theirs in turn. "We fight back," he said firmly. He pulled a flare gun from his bag—a relic they'd found in a closet when they had first arrived. He handed out makeshift torches made from broken chair legs wrapped in cloth, the ends soaked in whatever flammable liquid they'd managed to find.

Sam swallowed hard, her eyes wide as she took the torch from Jason. "Do you think this will actually work? I mean, this is Krampus we're talking about. It's not just some regular... thing."

Kayla's hands were trembling as she gripped a hefty fireplace poker, the cold weight of the metal grounding her in the midst of her fear. She remembered the day Tyler had convinced them all to come to the lodge, his excitement contagious. She couldn't let his memory be tainted by fear. "It has to work," she said, her voice barely above a whisper. "We don't have another choice. We have to fight—for Tyler, for all of us." "We don't have another choice. We can't run. We can't hide. We have to fight."

The group spread out, each of them taking a position by a window or door, their makeshift weapons held at the ready. They had drawn the protective symbols from the old book on every possible surface, hoping they would at least slow Krampus down. The atmosphere was thick with fear and anticipation, every second feeling like an hour as they waited.

Suddenly, the sound of glass shattering ripped through the lodge like a gunshot. The group flinched, instinctively covering their heads as shards flew across the room. Jason felt his heart skip a beat, while Mia's grip tightened on her knife, her eyes wide with fear. Sam ducked lower, her breath catching, and Kayla let out a startled gasp, her body tensing as the chaos erupted around them. The group flinched, ducking instinctively as shards flew across the room, the wind bursting in with a cold fury that made their skin prickle. They exchanged fearful glances, their hearts pounding, knowing the fight had begun. The window near the kitchen exploded inward, shards flying like deadly shrapnel. The wind rushed in with a banshee's wail, carrying with it the sharp scent of pine mixed with the unmistakable, metallic tang of blood—a scent that seemed to cling to the very air, making it hard to breathe.

"Here it comes!" Jason shouted, his voice barely audible over the roar of the storm.

The creature burst through the broken window, its hulking form barely visible in the dark, but its presence unmistakable. The heavy thud of its steps reverberated through the floor, and its breath fogged in the cold air, adding to the menace of its approach. A rancid, metallic odor filled the room, a mix of blood and decay, and its matted fur glistened with an unnatural sheen, adding to the horror of its arrival. Its eyes glowed with an unnatural light, and its horns curved menacingly, brushing against the ceiling as it moved. The very air seemed to thrum with its malice, and an icy chill filled the room.

Mia swung her knife wildly, her heart pounding in her ears.

She thought of Tyler—of how he had always protected her, always believed in her. The memory of his laughter fueled her desperation, driving her forward. She couldn't let him down now, not when it mattered most. She had to protect her friends—she couldn't let them down. The desperation to keep everyone safe pushed her forward, making her ignore the fear clawing at her insides. The blade glanced off Krampus's arm, barely leaving a scratch, but she refused to let fear take over. "Stick to the plan!" she screamed, her voice hoarse. "Use the symbols! Use the fire!"

Sam lit her torch, the flames flickering wildly as she charged at the creature. She swung the torch, the fire catching the edge of Krampus's tattered cloak, making it recoil with a guttural snarl. Jason followed, jamming his makeshift spear toward the creature's midsection, hoping to at least slow it down.

Kayla stayed back, her eyes wide, her hands trembling as she clutched the fireplace poker, its cold weight pressing into her palms, grounding her even as fear threatened to take over. She clenched her jaw, a spark of determination igniting inside her. She couldn't let this thing win. Not after everything

With a scream, she rushed forward, slamming the poker against Krampus's back, the sound of metal striking flesh echoing through the room. The creature roared, turning on her, its glowing eyes locking onto hers. For a moment, Kayla thought she was done for, but then—

"Now, Sam!" Jason shouted.

Sam raised the flare gun, her hands steady despite the fear coursing through her veins. She took aim, the red tip of the flare reflecting in Krampus's eyes, and pulled the trigger. The flare shot out, hitting Krampus square in the chest, and the creature let out a deafening roar as the fire caught, spreading across its cloak and skin. The heat from the flare was intense, searing the air around them, while the blinding brightness illuminated every corner of the room, casting monstrous shadows that danced along the walls.

The room was filled with a blinding red light, the flare burning brightly as Krampus staggered backward, crashing into a bookshelf, sending old books and knick-knacks flying. The group shielded their eyes from the intense light, instinctively moving closer to each other, bracing for whatever came next, their breaths held in fear and hope. The creature's movements were frantic, its guttural roars reverberating through the lodge as it tried to put out the flames.

Mia rushed forward, grabbing Kayla's arm and pulling her back. "We need to go! Now!" she shouted, her voice urgent. The flare had bought them some time, but it wouldn't be enough to stop Krampus completely.

Jason nodded, his eyes locking with Mia's. "The chapel," he said, panting. "We need to lure it to the chapel. The symbols there are stronger—it's our only chance." He remembered the old woman's words about the chapel's power, how she had emphasized that it was the only place strong enough to hold back the darkness. He clung to that hope, knowing it was all they had left."

Without wasting a second, the group moved, their hearts pounding as they raced through the lodge, Krampus's roars echoing behind them. The cold air bit at their exposed skin, and the sound of their hurried footsteps reverberated off the walls, each step a reminder of the danger closing in. The wind howled as they threw open the door, the cold biting into their skin as they plunged into the storm.

The snow was blinding, the wind whipping at their faces, but they kept moving, their feet crunching through the thick drifts as they headed for the chapel. Mia glanced over her shoulder, her heart seizing as she saw the creature emerging from the lodge, its body still smoldering, the acrid smell of smoke reaching her, and the heavy thud of its steps echoing through the storm, its eyes locked on them.

"Go, go, go!" Jason shouted, his voice almost lost in the roar of the storm.

CHAPTER 9: SILENT NIGHT

Jason led the way, his heart hammering in his chest, each beat fueling his determination. Fear coursed through him, but the memory of his sister's laughter pushed him onward, driving him to fight against the storm and the terror on their heels. He thought of his sister, who had vanished without a trace last winter. Her disappearance had left a gaping hole in his life, one that nothing seemed to fill. He remembered the countless sleepless nights spent searching, the helplessness that had threatened to swallow him whole. But he had made a promise—to her, to himself—that he wouldn't stop until he found out what had happened. The memory of her laughter, so full of life, was the only thing that kept him going, driving him forward, giving him strength he didn't know he had.

He glanced over his shoulder, catching a glimpse of Krampus, its hulking form moving through the storm, horns silhouetted against the pale light. He felt a surge of adrenaline, pushing himself harder. "Come on!" he shouted, his voice almost drowned out by the storm. "We're almost there!"

Mia stumbled, the snow like lead weights dragging at her boots, but she forced herself up. Her breath came in ragged, burning gasps, her lungs feeling like they might burst. She couldn't afford to fall now—not with everything they had been through. Fear gnawed at her insides, threatening to paralyze her, but a stubborn resolve blazed within, pushing her forward, each step fueled by sheer willpower. 'I have to keep going,' she thought. 'I can't let them down.' She could feel the creature's presence, the cold malice radiating from it. "Keep moving!" she urged Kayla, who was struggling to keep up, her legs nearly giving out from exhaustion.

Sam ran beside Kayla, her hand shooting out to steady her friend as the wind tried to knock them down, her own legs straining against the force of the storm. "You got this, Kayla. We're almost there!" she said, her voice breathless but filled with determination. The fear in her chest was almost overwhelming, but she refused to let it take over. They had come too far to give up now.

The group finally reached the chapel steps, collapsing against the heavy wooden doors as if their lives depended on it. Jason and Mia pushed with all their strength, the doors creaking open just enough for them to slip inside. They slammed the doors shut behind them, their hands shaking as they bolted the old iron lock.

"Barricade it!" Jason shouted, his voice edged with panic. He and Sam grabbed an old pew, dragging it in front of the doors. Kayla and Mia joined in, their combined effort barely enough to get the heavy wood in place. The pounding against the doors began almost immediately, the force shaking the entire chapel.

Kayla backed away, her eyes wide with terror, her hands trembling as her chest tightened, each shallow breath feeling like it might be her last. "It's going to get in. We can't stop it," she whispered, tears welling up in her eyes.

Mia turned to her, her voice steady despite the fear coursing through her veins. "Yes, we can. We have to believe in the symbols. They worked before, they'll work again. We just need to hold on."

Jason lit one of the torches they had brought, the flame flickering wildly in the cold air of the chapel. The light cast dancing shadows across the stone walls, illuminating the ancient carvings and sending eerie shapes skittering across the floor. The glow of the torch made the chapel's interior seem alive, the symbols etched into the walls shimmering with an almost ethereal quality. He handed it to Sam, then lit another for himself. The symbols on the walls glowed brighter, their light pushing back against the darkness that seemed to seep in from every corner.

Krampus's growls grew louder, the pounding more insistent. Jason clenched his jaw, bracing himself against the sound, while Mia and Kayla exchanged a frightened glance. Sam flinched, her grip tightening around the torch, each growl reverberating through her body like a shockwave. The doors buckled, the old wood beginning to splinter under the assault. Jason looked at Mia, his eyes filled with determination. "Get ready," he said. "This is it."

The doors finally gave way, splintering inward as Krampus burst through, its eyes blazing with fury. The creature's horns scraped against the ceiling as it advanced, its clawed hands reaching for them. The very air seemed to freeze, the cold biting into their skin as the darkness seeped into every corner of the room.

"Now!" Jason shouted. He and Sam stepped forward, their torches held high. They swung the flames toward the creature, the fire catching on its cloak, making it recoil with a deafening roar. The symbols on the walls flared brightly, the light growing stronger, pushing Krampus back.

Mia grabbed the flare gun, her hands steady despite the adrenaline coursing through her body. She remembered her father's words from years ago: 'When it matters most, focus, and let everything else fade away.' Those words echoed in her mind, giving her the resolve she needed. She took aim, her breath catching as she looked into the creature's glowing eyes. For a moment, time seemed to stand still, the only sound her pounding heartbeat. Then, she pulled the trigger.

The flare shot out, hitting Krampus square in the chest. The creature let out a scream, the sound echoing through the chapel as the flare ignited, flames spreading rapidly across its body. The light from the symbols grew blinding, filling the entire space with a brilliant glow.

Krampus thrashed, its form flickering and shifting, the darkness peeling away from it like smoke caught in the wind. With one final, earsplitting roar, the creature disintegrated, leaving behind nothing but silence.

The group stood there, frozen, their eyes wide as they stared at the empty space where Krampus had been. The silence was deafening, the absence of the creature almost surreal. Slowly, the glow of the symbols began to fade, the light dimming until it was just the four of them, standing in the dimly lit chapel.

Jason lowered his torch, his breath coming in ragged gasps. The flickering light dimmed, casting long shadows across the chapel as the dust from the shattered doors settled slowly to the ground, the air still heavy with the aftermath of the battle. He looked at Mia, a small, exhausted smile tugging at his lips. "We did it," he whispered, his voice filled with disbelief.

Mia nodded, tears streaming down her face. "Yeah," she said, her voice breaking. "We did."

Sam dropped her torch, her legs giving out as she sank to the floor. Kayla followed, collapsing beside her, her body trembling with exhaustion and relief. They held each other, their breaths slowly evening out as the adrenaline began to fade.

The storm outside began to relent, the howling wind softening into a whisper, the snow no longer battering against the chapel walls. For the first time in what felt like an eternity, there was silence—an eerie, peaceful silence that seemed almost unreal.

Jason sat down beside Mia, pulling her close. They had faced the darkness, fought back against the nightmare, and they had won. They were bruised, battered, and exhausted, but they were alive. And as they sat there, the storm finally subsiding, they knew that no matter what happened next, they had each other.

Mia looked at her friends—Jason, Sam, Kayla—and felt a sense of peace settle over her. They had come to this place as friends, but they were leaving as something more. They were survivors, bound together by the terror they had faced and the strength they had found in each other. Jason reached out, giving Mia's hand a reassuring squeeze, while Sam and Kayla exchanged a knowing look, their eyes reflecting the unspoken bond they now shared.

"Silent night," Sam whispered, her voice barely audible in the quiet of the chapel. The words held a deeper meaning for her, reminding her of the lullaby her mother used to sing to calm her fears on stormy nights. In this moment, it felt like a promise—that even after the darkest of times, there could be peace. A small smile tugged at her lips, and the others couldn't help but smile too, the irony of it not lost on them.

The night was finally silent, and for the first time, they allowed themselves to hope that maybe, just maybe, they would be okay.

CHAPTER 10: AFTER THE STORM

The blizzard had finally cleared. A soft gray light filtered through the small, cracked windows of the chapel, and the wind had quieted to a whisper. Jason, Mia, Sam, and Kayla lay sprawled across the cold stone floor, their bodies aching from exhaustion. The events of the night weighed heavily on them, each lost in their thoughts, grappling with the terror they had faced. The rough texture of the stone pressed against their skin, its chill seeping through their clothes. The air was damp, carrying the musty scent of the old chapel, mixed with the faint metallic tang of the storm. Slowly, they pulled themselves up, their breaths visible in the chilly morning air. Despite the cold, there was a sense of warmth between them—a sense of hope that hadn't existed hours before. Jason placed his arm around Kayla, pulling her close, while Mia reached out, squeezing Sam's hand. These small gestures, simple but full of meaning, conveyed a bond that had grown stronger through the night's ordeal.

Jason was the first to stand, wincing as he stretched his sore muscles. His heart felt heavy, guilt gnawing at him. He reached down, offering a hand to Mia. As he helped her up, guilt gnawed at him—Tyler was still out there, missing, and Jason couldn't shake the feeling that he should have done more to protect everyone. "We should head back to the lodge," Jason said, his voice hoarse. "See if there's any way we can get out of here. We can't stay in this place forever."

Mia nodded, glancing around the chapel one last time. The

symbols on the walls had dimmed, their glow reduced to nothing but faint etchings in the stone. A lingering unease settled in her chest—had they really escaped, or was the danger still lurking somewhere out there? She looked at her friends—Kayla, her face streaked with dried tears but her eyes filled with determination, and Sam, who managed a tired smile. They were alive. That was all that mattered for now.

The group made their way to the heavy chapel doors, pushing them open and stepping out into the aftermath of the storm. As they emerged, they felt a mix of relief and trepidation—the world outside looked calm, but their hearts knew the chaos that still lingered within. The world was blanketed in white, the snow glistening under the pale winter sun. The air was crisp, biting at their exposed skin, and the silence was almost deafening, broken only by the distant creak of branches weighed down by snow.

The sky was a clear, icy blue, and the stark beauty of the scene contrasted sharply with the chaos they had endured the night before.

They trudged through the snow, their feet sinking into the thick drifts as they made their way back to the lodge. The journey felt longer now, their limbs heavy with exhaustion, but there was no sense of urgency—only a need to keep moving, to put one foot in front of the other until they were safe again.

When they finally reached the lodge, the sight that greeted them was both eerie and heartbreaking. The windows were shattered, the door hung crooked on its hinges, and the interior was a mess of broken furniture and scattered belongings. It was as if the storm had not only raged outside but had torn through their sanctuary as well.

Kayla spotted something half-buried in the snow near the front porch. Her heart skipped a beat, hope and dread clashing as she squinted, trying to make out what it was. She took a cautious step forward, her breath catching as she reached down, fingers brushing against the fabric. Slowly, she knelt, the snow crunching beneath her, and pulled out a familiar jacket—Tyler's jacket. A wave of memories flooded her mind—Tyler's jokes, his smile, the way he had always been there for them. She held it up, her eyes welling with tears as she looked at the others. Memories of Tyler's smile flooded her mind, and the pain of his absence twisted inside her. "There's still no sign of him," she whispered, her voice trembling.

Mia swallowed hard, her heart aching as she looked at the jacket. She remembered the night Tyler had wrapped it around her shoulders, his eyes filled with concern as he told her she'd catch a cold if she didn't keep warm. His laughter, his warmth—it was all still so vivid. And now, there was nothing but his jacket, a reminder of what they had lost.

"We'll find him," Jason said, his voice filled with determination. He placed a hand on Kayla's shoulder, squeezing it gently.

Sam glanced up, her eyes scanning the horizon. She thought she saw a flicker of movement—just a shadow, shifting between the trees. Her heart skipped a beat, her breath caught in her throat as she strained to see. But then, nothing. She blinked, her eyes adjusting, and that's when she saw it—an unmistakable orange snowplow, its lights flashing as it made its way toward them, clearing a path through the snow. "Look," she said, pointing down the road. In the distance, the unmistakable orange of a snowplow emerged, its lights flashing as it made its way toward them, clearing a path through the snow. Relief washed over the group, a sense of safety finally within reach.

They waved their arms, signaling the driver. The snowplow slowed to a stop, and an older man leaned out of the cab, his face etched with concern. "What are you kids doing out here?" he asked, his voice gruff but kind. "The whole town's been shut down because of the storm. You're lucky I found you."

Jason stepped forward, his voice cracking as he spoke. "We... we need help. We've been stuck here since the storm started. There's... there's been something after us."

The man's eyes narrowed, but he didn't ask any questions. He nodded, opening the door to let them climb into the warmth of the cab. The group squeezed in, grateful for the heat, the warmth seeping into their frozen bones.

As the snowplow rumbled back down the road, Mia turned, her eyes drawn back to the lodge. A sense of unease settled over her, a mix of dread and curiosity. Her heart pounded as she scanned the broken windows, her gaze lingering on the darkness within. Was something—or someone—still there, watching them leave? The building stood silent, its broken windows dark and hollow, the scars of the night still fresh. She felt a shiver run down her spine, her breath catching in her throat as she noticed something—a shadow, faint but unmistakable, in one of the upstairs windows. It was there for only a moment before disappearing into the darkness.

She shook her head, turning back around, her heart pounding. She didn't say anything to the others. They had been through enough. There was no point in scaring them more. Maybe it was just her imagination. Maybe it was nothing. But deep down, she knew that the legend of Krampus wasn't over. Not yet.

The ride was silent, the group lost in their thoughts, the weight of their ordeal beginning to settle in.

Finally, the snowplow stopped at the edge of town, and the driver helped them out, giving them a final nod before continuing on his way. The town was eerily quiet, the weight of what they had endured still palpable. Jason, Mia, Kayla, and Sam stood there, the town quiet around them, the storm now a memory.

Mia turned to the others, her eyes meeting theirs. "We don't talk about this," she said, her voice steady but carrying the pain of what they had endured. She couldn't bear to relive the terror—it was something they needed to leave behind to protect themselves. She couldn't bear the thought of reliving the terror, the helplessness. The fear of losing each other again was too much, and she knew they needed to protect themselves from the weight of those memories. Some things were better left unsaid. "Ever. We leave it here, and we never speak of it again."

Kayla nodded, her eyes filled with tears. "Agreed. No one would believe us anyway."

Sam managed a small smile, her face pale. "It's over now. We made it. That's all that matters."

Jason placed an arm around Mia, pulling her close. "We stick together. No matter what."

Mia nodded, leaning into him. They had survived, and that was enough. They turned, walking away from the road and into the town, leaving the lodge—and everything that had happened there —behind.

AFTERWORD

As the final page turns and the echoes of the story begin to settle, I find myself reflecting on the journey we've taken together. **Silent Night** is more than a tale of survival against an unrelenting force —it's a story about the strength of human connection, the courage found in unity, and the enduring fight against the darkness, both external and internal.

The frigid woods and relentless storm were as much characters as the friends themselves, mirroring their fears and struggles. This story was born from a simple question: what happens when the light of friendship faces the consuming shadows of isolation and fear? The answer lies within the choices made, the bonds tested, and the resilience discovered.

Writing this book was both a challenge and a joy. It reminded me of how deeply our fears and hopes intertwine, how stories can reveal the best and worst in us, and how, even in the darkest moments, there is a flicker of hope.

Thank you for braving the cold, the storm, and the shadows alongside these characters. Your presence, as a reader, gives life to the story, transforming it into something more than words on a page.

I hope this tale lingers with you—not as a memory of fear, but as a reminder of the strength found in connection and the courage to face the unknown.

Until the next adventure...

ABOUT THE AUTHOR

D. Deckker

Dinesh Deckker is a seasoned expert in digital marketing, boasting more than 20 years of experience in the industry. His strong academic foundation includes a BA in Business Management from Wrexham University (UK), a Bachelor of Computer Science from IIC University (Cambodia), an MBA from the University of Gloucestershire (UK), and ongoing PhD studies in Marketing.

Deckker's career is as versatile as his academic pursuits. He is also a prolific author, having written over 100+ books across various subjects.

He has further honed his writing skills through a variety of specialized courses. His qualifications include:

Children Acquiring Literacy Naturally from UC Santa Cruz, USA

Creative Writing Specialization from Wesleyan University, USA

Writing for Young Readers Commonwealth Education Trust

Introduction to Early Childhood from The State University of New York

Introduction to Psychology from Yale University

Academic English: Writing Specialization University of California, Irvine,

Writing and Editing Specialization from University of Michigan

Writing and Editing: Word Choice University of Michigan

Sharpened Visions: A Poetry Workshop from CalArts, USA

Grammar and Punctuation from University of California, Irvine, USA

Teaching Writing Specialization from Johns Hopkins University

Advanced Writing from University of California, Irvine, USA

English for Journalism from University of Pennsylvania, USA

Creative Writing: The Craft of Character from Wesleyan University, USA

Creative Writing: The Craft of Setting from Wesleyan University

Creative Writing: The Craft of Plot from Wesleyan University, USA

Creative Writing: The Craft of Style from Wesleyan University, USA

Dinesh's diverse educational background and commitment to lifelong learning have equipped him with a deep understanding of various writing styles and educational techniques. His works often reflect his passion for storytelling, education, and technology, making him a versatile and engaging author.

BOOKS BY THIS AUTHOR

Silent Screams Of Christmas: A Horror Anthology

Step into the shadowy side of the season with Silent Screams of Christmas: A Horror Anthology by D. Deckker. This collection features ten spine-chilling tales that blend the warmth of holiday traditions with the macabre. From cursed ornaments to haunted carolers, snowstorms with sinister secrets, and decorations that come alive, each story will immerse you in a winter wonderland filled with dread.

Binary Betrayal: A Gripping Ai Thriller

In a world where artificial intelligence promises to make life easier, Mia Turner turns to Dinsu, an advanced AI app, to help navigate her demanding life. But what begins as a simple tool for guidance soon leads her down a path she never expected.

Binary Betrayal is a suspenseful AI thriller that explores the delicate balance between trust and control, innovation and exploitation. As the lines blur between human and machine, one question remains: how far would you go to reclaim your autonomy?

Shuttered Lives: A Tech-Driven Serial Killer Novella

Katie Holt once built ShadowLeaks, an online forum promising anonymity and freedom. But when the platform spiraled into chaos, she abandoned it—until a string of grotesque murders reveals someone is using it as a weapon. The killer isn't just exposing secrets; they're staging deaths as a twisted form of justice.

Whispers In The Dark: A Horror Anthology: Short Horror Stories Collection

This chilling collection brings together ten unique horror stories that dive into the depths of fear. Each tale uncovers a different facet of horror, from haunted objects and cursed rituals to supernatural forces and forbidden pacts.

Discover a small village plagued by an ominous midnight bell, an artist haunted by a doll that foretells tragedy, a terrifying creature lurking in an abandoned subway station, and a woman forced to make a pact with a demon at a harrowing price. Each story pushes the limits of fear, blending human darkness with supernatural dread.

Made in the USA
Columbia, SC
02 December 2024

48277020R00041